GUYLA ADAMS

The Dragon of Happy Tails
Carter's Quest

First published by Guyla Adams 2025

Copyright © 2025 by Guyla Adams

All rights reserved. No part of this publication may be reproduced, stored or transmitted in any form or by any means, electronic, mechanical, photocopying, recording, scanning, or otherwise without written permission from the publisher. It is illegal to copy this book, post it to a website, or distribute it by any other means without permission.

This novel is entirely a work of fiction. The names, characters and incidents portrayed in it are the work of the author's imagination. Any resemblance to actual persons, living or dead, events or localities is entirely coincidental.

Guyla Adams asserts the moral right to be identified as the author of this work.

Designations used by companies to distinguish their products are often claimed as trademarks. All brand names and product names used in this book and on its cover are trade names, service marks, trademarks and registered trademarks of their respective owners. The publishers and the book are not associated with any product or vendor mentioned in this book. None of the companies referenced within the book have endorsed the book.

First edition

This book was professionally typeset on Reedsy.
Find out more at reedsy.com

To my amazing grandkids—
You are the sparkle in my eyes and the laughter in my heart.
May you always dream big, believe boldly, and know that the greatest adventures begin with faith, courage, and kindness. Love Grandma
Remember, you were made for wonderful things.
"Put on the full armor of God, so that you can take your stand against the devil's schemes.
Stand firm then, with the belt of truth buckled around your waist, with the breastplate of righteousness in place." Ephesians 6:10-18

Contents

Acknowledgments	ii
Introduction	1
The Sparkle at Happy Tails	3
The Midnight Zoo	7
The Mirror Lake & The Bracelet of Light	13
The Clock Tower of Faithfulness	20
Library of Whispers	27
The Colosseum in the Sky	33
Falls of kindness	39
The Carnival at the Carousel	46
The Mansion of Forgotten Echoes	57
The Art of Creativity	63
The New Dream	70
About the Author	76
Also by Guyla Adams	78

Acknowledgments

Acknowledgments First off, a giant thank you to my son, Kaden Adams, who patiently helped me sort through some wild ideas, tamed them into stories, and occasionally reminded me that sleep is, in fact, important.

To my friends Pamela Lopez and Cindy Vaughan—your encouragement, feedback, and "you've got this!" pep talks kept me going more than coffee ever could (and that's saying something). To my mom Connie for standing by me no matter what. A special shout-out to Neelan Adams and Jackie Hansen for the art advice- you saved me from some truly questionable dragon doodles.

Finally to my big, wonderful family: thank you for letting me steal hours, days, and sometimes entire weekends to chase words and dreams. Your patience, love, and support gave me the wings to finish this. If you ever wondered why dinner was Costco pizza again… well, now you know.

Introduction

For the Dreamers, the Quiet Ones, and the Kids with Big Wings, Even if They Can't See Them Yet.

This story is for every kid who's ever felt a little different. For the ones who stare out windows during math class, wondering what clouds taste like. For the ones who build dragon lairs out of blankets. For the ones who whisper big ideas into their pillows at night. This story is for the ones who feel invisible sometimes. Or too loud. Or too quiet. Or like they don't quite fit inside the boxes other people expect them to.

Carter Jamyson felt that way, too. He wasn't the star of the class. He didn't win the races or ace the spelling bees. But he saw things-things other kids didn't. And when he found a shimmering glass dragon tucked away in a thrift store called Happy Tails, something extraordinary happened. He didn't just grow wings. He grew patience, joy, peace, kindness, love, goodness, faithfulness, gentleness, and self-control.

He grew into someone who knew his story mattered. This book is about magical lotion and moonlit adventure, sure. But it's also about the kind of magic that's already inside you, the kind that helps you believe in yourself, even when it's hard, especially when it's hard. So if you've ever wished for a dragon of your own, or hoped for a sign that you belong in this big, strange, beautiful world, this story is for you. Keep your heart and mind open. Keep your sense of adventure ready and never stop believing in the impossible.

See you in the sky,

The Storytellers Behind the Scales

The Sparkle at Happy Tails

Nine-year-old Carter Jamyson was pretty sure Saturdays were magic. Not because there was no school, although that helped, but because it was the only day his mom would let him wander around Happy Tails, the quirkiest, weirdest, and most wonderful thrift shop in all of Hollow Creek, Maridale.

Happy Tails wasn't just a standard antique store, full of old mugs and forgotten lava lamps. When Carter wandered the many nooks and crannies of the store, it was full of possibilities. In the past, he had discovered pirate maps hidden behind old dusty books and old coins from origins unknown. While exploring the store, sometimes he swore he could feel a warm presence guiding him to his next big discovery.

On this particular Saturday, he was browsing the cluttered back shelves littered with miscellaneous items. Suddenly, a bright flash of light filled the room. When he glanced towards the direction of the light, he saw something shimmering, almost radiating- from deep within. He gasped. Another shopper glanced his way.

Carter gave a shy smile, not wanting to draw any attention. He stole a glance down the aisle where his mom was elbows-deep in her eternal hunt for "that heather-gray sweater with the leather toggle buttons, she loved in high school," lost long ago. Oblivious of his discovery.

When the other customer returned to their own bargain hunting, Carter cautiously approached the area where the flash of light came from. There, he saw a partially covered item, slowly removing the silk cloth that concealed it. The first thing he noticed was the shape of a mythical creature called a dragon. This dragon didn't growl or breathe fire, though. The dragon appeared to be made of a glass-like material that Carter had never seen. The dragon was curled delicately on a faded blue silk pillow. Its surface shimmered with every color imaginable, mostly purple, with hints of green, blue, and gold. It sparkled like twinkling stars. Carter felt something deep in his belly, flutter, like the moment you reach the top of a roller coaster and you're about to plunge down to the bottom.

He had to have it.

Carter quickly snatched up the dragon, which was delicate but surprisingly heavy, and handed it to the store clerk. After a harsh negotiation involving a crumpled five dollar bill and his most sincere puppy-dog eyes, the dragon was his.

Later that night, as the sun put itself to rest behind the surrounding mountains, the stars began to shine, and the wind began to playfully tap on the window. Huddled under a blanket with only a flashlight at his disposal, he began to deeply inspect the dragon. While running his hand across the smooth surface of the dragon, his hand discovered a small star shape on the dragon's leg. Carter placed his flashlight between his neck and shoulder to further inspect the star. When it suddenly compressed beneath his fingers, a small, quiet click echoed through the room. A square compartment on the base of the dragon suddenly appeared out of nowhere and opened, revealing a mysterious container.

Inside the mysterious container was a thick, shimmering lotion that glowed faintly under the flashlight's glow. There was an ancient, tattered paper attached to the neck of the bottle that read:

"Use sparingly. For shoulders only. May cause elevation." "May cause elevation?"

Carter whispered, squinting. "What does that mean?" He thought. Curiosity took over. Carter had to know what this mysterious lotion did. He dipped his finger into the lotion, shrugged, and rubbed a little on each shoulder. Carter was overwhelmed with excitement and filled with curiosity.

As the lotion began to absorb into his skin, he began to worry.

"Nothing..." Disappointed, Neil threw off the blanket that enclosed him. He put down the flashlight and retreated to the window to see the bottles' tattered instructions in the light of the full moon. As Carter approached the window with the mysterious bottle and the glass dragon, everything changed. The glass dragon appeared to absorb the moonlight, and the whole room was enveloped in a bright white light. Carter frantically covered his eyes, curling into a ball. Suddenly, an overwhelming energy took over his entire body, specifically the energy felt like it was flowing toward his shoulder blades. Carter began to see bright sparks of light in every color like fireworks, even through his closed eyes. The feeling of strength overwhelmed his body, and he began to stand, feeling lighter than he ever had before. The lights began to fade, and he had regained the strength to open his eyes.

Upon opening his eyes, Carter found himself floating in the air at least a foot off the ground; he also felt a strong wind blowing through his room. Carter's back had sprouted two wings reaching six feet in length, covered with the purest white scales he had ever seen. They were gems that sparkled like diamonds. He gasped, but not in fear, in awe. Wearing a grin that stretched from ear to ear, he threw the window wide open and dove through it as if he had done it a thousand times before. He was exhilarated with pure "Joy!" Never had he fully experienced this feeling until now.

He began to fall.

The Midnight Zoo

Carter began plummeting toward the ground, but there was no fear in his heart. The massive six-foot angelic wings spread wide open, catching the cool midnight breeze, lifting him high into the night sky. The night sky was empty and dark, allowing Carter to truly experience and savor the journey ahead of him. With closed eyes, he could truly feel the deep "Whoosh" sounds his magnificent wings created, while displacing the air, allowing him to move freely. The feeling of the cool crisp air dancing around his body, forcing his clothes to rustle against his skin.

During this moment, an extreme sense of freedom and anticipation took over Carter's entire body, and he began to shake with excitement.

For the first time, he was ready to truly appreciate his hometown. Hollow Creek's homes lit up the night sky, illuminating most intensely near his desired destination. Sweet memories flooded Carter's mind, and he began to experience a sense of euphoria. Memories of a time spent with his bearded grandfather who he knew was secretly Santa and his sweet grandmother, who was most definitely Mrs. Claus. The time between visits always felt too far away. The most cherished memories since their last visit were the time they spent at the zoo and when they bought their family a membership, so they could continue to cherish the memory.

Carter began to feel a pull at his heart, and unconsciously, his wings began to pick up speed. Thoughts of the zoo buzzing with life during the day, school field trips with loads of kids spilling over the sidewalks like a roaring river. There is always an overwhelming aroma of buttery popcorn hanging thick in the air, and one mischievous goat in the animal petting section, continuing his never ending mission to devour the shoelaces of all that enter. Carter had walked these paths many times before, hands tucked into his pockets, quietly watching while other kids pointed and giggled.

He knew well what the zoo had in store during day excursions, but what awaited him during the night? From the sky, the vast array of paths and large exhibits of the zoo became more and more clear as Carter began to make his descent. His eyes were set on a winding path stretching through many exhibits, focused on the path ahead. Carter stretched out his wings, furrowing them to slow himself for a soft landing. As the path quickly approached, a sudden change in the wind forced him off course, throwing him onto a high mound inside an enclosure.

Slightly dazed, he assessed the damage and was overjoyed as he had not incurred any injuries. He took a deep sigh of relief, "Phew!" A loud sound of violent, deep banging broke the silence. He peered toward the direction of the disruptive sound and was overcome with dread. A large dark shadow loomed over him and was violently striking its chest with its massive fists. The enormous creature began to approach him. The distance between Carter and the massive dark animal shrank drastically when a massive golden feline creature intercepted the path of the large dark animal. The two animals collided, and the large black animal was forced off course, landing on its back. Carter sat in awe as he observed the imposing golden animal. It was a majestic lion. The King of the jungle began to shake off the impact and let out a bone-shaking "ROAR." Now that the immediate danger had subsided, Carter recognized the large dark animal as a gorilla. The gorilla, named Goliath, glared at the lion and yelled in a deep, thundering voice, "You may have bested me this time, but next time you will not be the *Victor.*"

Then the lion blinked at Carter once, twice, slowly, admiring his magnificent wings, which were huddled tight to his back. The lion had a distant memory recalling similar visitors in the past with magnificent wings. Carter froze. His heart did a somersault inside his chest. He locked eyes with the lion, who began to lounge on a nearby rock, examining Carter closely. As the lion began to stand again, his muscles began rippling beneath his fur, and he stretched his huge body, resembling a house cat with a bountiful mane. The lion finally acknowledged Carter's existence, speaking to him with a soft, deep voice, "It's about time you showed up. Wings, huh?" the lion said, with a tone halfway between impressed and nostalgic. "Haven't seen those in a while." Carter's jaw nearly hit the concrete.

Once he regained his composure, Carter said, "Wait… you can talk?" The lion chuckled, a low, gravelly sound. "Of course I can talk. I'm a lion, I have thoughts, feelings, and opinions. Though humans rarely bother to ask. But you… You're listening. You're open. So, yes, you can hear me." The lion's demeanor drastically changed, becoming more rigid as he looked at the high walls and the body of water enclosing them. In a low, deep voice, the lion spoke, "Now comes the hard part." The lion directly addressed the strange boy with wings, "breaking into the exhibit was no challenge, but now I need your help to get out. Any ideas?"

Carter pondered the conundrum for a moment and stated abruptly, "I know what we must do." The plan began to take fruition, and Carter took a kneeling position with his wings stretched wide at the base of the water, eyes focused on the tall wall before them. From the far end of the exhibit, the lion began running, his deep, long strides reaching his top speed as the cool night air whipped through his long mane. Once he was within ten feet of the boy, the lion bellowed, "NOW!"

Carter sprang into action, forcing his body off the ground using all of his strength, forcing his wing down, and lifting his body up into the air. The lion took a massive leap straight at the boy. With upward momentum, Carter flattened his back, creating a platform for the lion to use as a stepping stone to clear the many barriers that obstructed their escape. The lion's front and back paws landed on Carter's back, and with all of his might, the lion pushed himself off of Carter and cleared all the obstacles and achieved freedom. Carter continued his upward momentum using his massive wings to defy gravity and soared over the barriers, lightly landing beside the lion.

The lion felt moved and astonished that the boy's plan had worked. The lion turned toward the boy and, in a low raspy voice, stated, "You know everyone looks up to me for answers and to take charge." The lion's voice softened and in a sincere tone said, "When we were trapped, I lost hope, I did not have a solution. You saved me and displayed courage like I have never seen before. I will strive to be like you."

Carter had a strange feeling throughout his body, which was unfamiliar to him. Thoughts flew through his mind: "You saved me", "Courage," and "I will strive to be like you." Carter had never associated himself with any of those words, let alone from someone as strong and powerful as the King of the Jungle. At a loss for words, Carter thoughtfully nodded at the lion and asked, "What is your name?" The lion said with great emotion, "Boy, my name is Orion. Now that we are safe, let's take a walk."

The full moon illuminated the pathways of the zoo, and the mood in the air changed. The lion and the brave boy began their walk. Carter had many questions for the lion regarding other winged visitors. What he knew of the ancient bottle from the Glass dragon, and how he knew Carter was coming to the zoo.

As if Orion had read Carter's mind, he stopped. He looked at the boy as if looking at his own cub. Carter knew he was safe in the lions' company. "You are not the first winged visitor we have received here in my home, but you certainly displayed something that I have never seen from the others," Orion said. Then continued, "I have seen many winged visitors throughout the years, most of them display hardship, and when they arrive, the zoo will shift to meet their challenge. Before your arrival, my cage door became unlocked, I felt the shift, and I knew you were coming."

Carter pondered the words that the lion spoke for a while and asked, "What do you know of a crystal dragon and its ancient bottle?"

Perplexed, the lion responded, "I know not of what you speak, Boy." More assertively, Orion stated to Carter, "I do know that those with wings are special. They do not fit in with the ones here during the day. I strongly advise you not to show your wings during the daylight, as I have never seen the winged ones other than at night."

Carter nodded in understanding.

Taking charge, he began exploring the zoo, accompanied by Orion. The animals were much more lively during the night, as opposed to the frequent slumbering they did during the day.

The wolves that Carter had never seen began playfully arguing back and forth regarding who was the strongest as they tugged on a rope, with all their might. The flamingos had synchronized movements, twirling their pink feathers around, and singing a majestic melody about a long flight to faraway places, almost as if rehearsing for a ballet.

Of his favorites, the penguins were having a full-on pool party. One was floating on its back like a vacationer, another was stealing fish from its buddy, and two more were racing in circles like kids hopped up on soda. Carter couldn't stop laughing. "You guys do this when the lights go out? No wonder you all look sleepy during the day!" The most shocking thing was when Carter saw a sloth swim faster than he had ever thought possible. As Carter wandered wide-eyed and smiling, the animals shared their stories.

Stories of other visitors who had once soared over the zoo with magical wings like his. Examples had been a boy who whistled lullabies to calm the wolves. A girl who used honey to mend the broken wings of an injured owl. Someone had once left a tiny, handwritten note wrapped around a pebble in the tortoise habitat that read: "Thank you for believing in me."

Carter's heart filled with love, warm and glowing, like the inside of a lantern. He wasn't just flying, he was part of something bigger. Something ancient and beautiful. Something secret and sacred. Neil felt a change in himself, feeling stronger. The boy stood, taking his massive six-foot angelic wings, spreading them wide, filling the scales with the night's cool breeze. The boy forced his wings down and back. With that, Carter was gone, leaving behind a single pure diamond scale.

The Mirror Lake & The Bracelet of Light

As Carter peeked out the window, it was just midnight. The early morning mist slithered through the trees like a sleepy serpent, curling around branches and rooftops. The world looked hushed, like it was holding its breath. Yet it whispered, "Something's coming…" Carter could feel it too. That sparkly flutter right in his chest, the kind that told him something magical was about to happen.

He didn't know where tonight's flight would take him. This was his first true midnight adventure. But something deep inside tugged at him, soft but also, like a compass tied to his heart. It told him, Follow the water.

"Guess that's the plan," he murmured, grinning.

Checklist time:

- *Lotion? Dabbed and rubbed in with care.*
- Wings? Not yet—but the shimmer had started, a ripple of light beneath his skin, like sunlight trapped underwater. Then came the tingle. A thousand tiny sparks danced across his shoulder blades. His back arched as something deep within him stretched awake. With a rush like sails catching wind, his wings burst forth, translucent, veined with colors too wild to name. They glimmered like stained glass catching firelight, the edges humming like a song. Pajamas? Still superhero themed, because obviously.

- Hoodie? Check: it was getting cold.

Carter grinned. "Ready for takeoff." He climbed onto the windowsill and leaped into the night. The air caught him instantly, crisp and cool. His wings sliced through the dark like silk, the moon pouring silver light over him.

He banked left, heading for the edge of town, destination: Mirror Lake. The wind brushed his cheeks. Below, the sleepy city is illuminated with faint streetlights. It felt like flying over a dream. But tonight felt different. The wind wasn't just carrying him; it was guiding him.

When he reached the lake, it stretched wide and still, a perfect mirror reflecting the stars. His mom always said it was "peaceful," the kind of place where your thoughts get quiet. A beautiful place to think and reflect. But Carter knew better.

At night, the lake wasn't peaceful. It was ancient. It remembered things. He dipped lower, wings trailing ripples across the surface.

Then, SPLASH! Carter froze. Another splash. A voice, a girl's voice, called out in panic. "Help! Please! Somebody!" Carter's heart jumped. He swooped toward the sound. On the far dock, a flashlight rolled across the boards, tumbling into the water. In the lake, someone was thrashing wildly.

Without hesitation, Carter dove.

"Hold on!" he shouted, wings slicing through the air. Cold water closed around him as he plunged in. He kicked hard, grabbed the girl's wrist, and pulled her up. With one powerful flap, his wings lifted them both from the lake, water streaming off like silver rain.

He landed on the dock and gently set her down. She coughed, gasped, her wet hair plastered to her face. Carter smiled, out of breath but calm. "Well, good thing I was flying by."

The girl blinked at him, shivering. "You have wings." Her voice trembled between disbelief and wonder.

He chuckled. "Yeah, they're kind of a limited-edition model. Haven't seen them in stores yet."

Despite herself, she laughed. "Are you... an angel or something?" "Not officially,"

Carter said, wringing water from his sleeve. "I'm still working on my Halo license." That got a bigger laugh, soft but real. "I'm Armi," she said between breaths. "Armi Wren."

"Carter Jamyson," he replied, offering a hand. "Nice to meet you, Armi, professional lake diver?"

Armi grinned, shaking his hand. "More like an accidental diver. My flashlight fell in, and I tried to grab it. Grandpa always says curiosity will get me in trouble."

"Curiosity is how people find magic," Carter said. "And, you know... deep lakes."

She tilted her head, studying him in the moonlight. "You talk like you've seen magic before."

Carter smiled. "I have. My wings are magic. I'm worried about what will happen when the magic runs out. As of right now, I am just enjoying the moment and seeing where the magic brings me. Like here, like tonight. The magic brought me to you."

The rain began to fall, soft and silvery. They both looked up, laughing as droplets sparkled in the glow of the moon. And that's when it happened, the air around them shimmered. A light pulsed in Carter's hands, swirling until it formed a glowing orb. Inside it, a word appeared:

Gentleness.

Carter stared. Another gift. The light pulsed softly, wrapping them both in warmth. And in that quiet glow, he understood something new: gentleness wasn't weakness. It was the strength to care when it mattered most.

Moments later, a flashlight beam cut through the mist. "Armi!" a man's voice cried. Her grandpa, James, came running down the path, tears of relief mixing with rain. He pulled her into his arms, holding her tight.

Carter stepped back into the trees. One last glance. One last smile. Then, with a whisper of his wings, he was gone. As he soared home, Carter pressed the glowing orb to his chest and whispered, "Even the smallest act can change someone's whole destiny." Above him, the stars seemed to delight in agreement.

And somewhere below, Armi whispered to her grandfather, "He had wings,

Grandpa. He saved me. Just like you said, magic finds kids who don't know how strong they are yet."

Dream Message

That night, Carter's dreams shimmered with color. He stood again by the lake, but now it glowed like liquid starlight. Ripples spread outward, and from the center rose a small glass jar, drifting toward him through the mist. Carter knelt beside the glowing water. Inside the jar gleamed a bracelet of white and gold.

"Armi..." he whispered.

When he touched the jar, warmth spread through him like sunlight on a cold morning. He heard her voice, faint but clear as if it was carried on the breeze:

"For my friend, Carter, the boy who flies."

The bracelet slipped free, wrapping gently around his wrist. It pulsed with soft golden light. Carter smiled, whispering, "I won't forget either."

When he woke, the morning sun poured through his window—and there it was. The bracelet. Real. Waiting.

He turned it in his fingers and laughed quietly. "Guess wishes really can travel far." Outside, the breeze stirred his curtains, carrying the scent of lake water and pine. Somewhere beyond the trees, Mirror Lake shimmered—as if smiling back.

The Bracelet of Light

That night, the rain had faded to a soft drizzle. Armi sat on her porch steps, a mug of cocoa steaming beside her and her grandpa's old tackle box open at her feet. Inside were tangled strings, beads, and bits of shiny thread, her crafting treasures. She picked out two cords of each color, one gold and one white.

"Grandpa," she said as her fingers worked, "do you think I really saw him?"

James looked up from his carving, a small wooden bird taking shape in his hands. "I think the world's a lot bigger than most folks realize," he said. "And you've always had eyes that see the in-between places."

Armi smiled a little, braiding the threads. "He saved me. I want to make him something. So if he ever comes back... he'll know I didn't forget."

The Dragon of Happy Tails

"Then make it strong," said James, "strong enough to carry a wish."

Armi tied off the ends. The bracelet shimmered faintly in the sunlight—white and gold threads glinting like the sun's reflection dancing on water. "For my friend, Carter," she whispered, "the boy who flies." She placed it in a tiny glass jar and set it on her windowsill, where the moonlight could find it.

That night, as the stars appeared, the bracelet pulsed softly—once, twice—like it was answering a call from far away. Carter held up his wrist, watching the bracelet glow faintly in the morning light. The threads shifted, gold melting into silver, white glinting like starlight.

For just a heartbeat, he thought he heard Armi's laughter echo through the wind. "See you again, friend," he whispered. And though the world outside looked perfectly ordinary, the air carried a whisper of magic. A playful gust lifted his curtains, brushing his face like a promise. Deep down, Carter knew this wasn't the end of their story.

It was only the beginning of a friendship written in the sky.

The Clock Tower of Faithfulness

Carter's eyes shot open, and he hastily threw his covers to the ground, bolting to his closet where the dragon was concealed. After pulling away the silk cloth, the dragon gleamed faintly in the moonlight. He pressed the hidden button, and with a soft shimmer, the ancient bottle appeared. He dabbed the lotion onto his shoulders, his heart racing with anticipation.

The dragon absorbed the moonlight, flooding his room in brilliance. He applied the lotion, preparing for the next adventure. Carter closed his eyes as the familiar euphoria coursed through him, energy surging through his body until his magnificent wings unfurled. Perched on the windowsill, he scanned the empty street below.

It had been nearly a week since his last flight. He dreamed of new places, and one shimmered brightest in his mind, the Historic Chippawa Town Hall is easily recognized by its large plate glass windows, and rooftop clock tower its heritage value in 1983 under City of Niagara Falls. It had been a place Carter had wanted to visit. He saw it once on a road trip with his parents. The old clock tower is located, in an older community situated, along the Niagara Falls' downtown. By day, it serves as a local community hub for residents of that southern section of the city, but at night, under the moon, it pulsed softly, almost like it had a heartbeat. It was calling him.

Carter leaped into the cool night sky, his wings guiding him like trusted friends. Stars winked above, and below, Hollow Creek slept. He landed gently on the ledge beneath the enormous clock face. Up close, the tower seemed alive. The wind curled around its spires with a sigh.

Tick. Tick. TICK.

The clock hands spun backward. A secret panel slid open, glowing gold. He observed the clock tower cautiously, running his hand across the face, ensuring the path was clear. With an unsure tone, Carter stated, "Here goes nothing!" He curled his wings up tight, wrapping them around his body. He leaped through the mysterious opening. Once clearing the opening, Carter witnessed a flash of green light revealing a large open space with a corridor leading down. Instinctively, the wings tightly wrapped around him, opening and catching air, allowing him to begin his descent. As he drifted down toward the green light, an unexpected gust of wind surged from beneath him.

It seemed as if the earth exhaled, stirred by the restless energy of an approaching storm or perhaps the heated breath of unseen forces rising from the ground. The air shimmered with tension, born from the distant shifting currents of a hidden world below, which began blowing beneath him. Inside, time unraveled. Golden gears twisted like vines, lanterns floated in slow motion, and shimmering orbs hovered in the air. Each one pulsed faintly, like captured heartbeats. Carter drifted between the orbs and lanterns.

As Carter drifted closer to the glowing balls of light, he noticed images flashing within the orbs. Viewing images of a child steadied his little sister's bike, letting go only when she laughed and pedaled on her own. In another, a man knelt to tie an old woman's shoe when her hands trembled too much. One glowed with a dog leaping into the arms of a soldier home from deployment. Another held a boy nervously standing up in class, telling the truth even though his voice cracked.

Carter observed that all the collective stories held within this mystical place displayed themes of kindness, courage, and love. Every orb appeared to be holding a memory of **faithfulness**, proof that time was stitched together by moments when people chose to care.

A tall man with well groomed hair, a thick beard, in a charcoal black overcoat and a matching top hat with simple wire glasses sitting upon his nose. With a warm smile, he greeted him with a bow. "Carter, right on time."

The Dragon of Happy Tails

Carter blinked. "How do you know my name?" "I'm Lowell, the Timekeeper," the man said warmly. "I've been watching your flight path. The penguins at the zoo speak highly of you."

Carter grinned. "You talk to the penguins?"

"Doesn't everyone?" Lowell replied with a grin. Lowell gestured warmly, drawing Carter's attention towards a particularly bright area within the walls of the tower. Carter felt a strong draw to take a step forward. As he began to walk, he heard the floor creaking and noticed heavy wear on the path he began to travel. As he looked farther forward, he saw a faint violet hue. Like clockwork, Lowell took the lead, guiding him deeper into the tower, where countless hourglasses glowed on floating shelves. Lowell gestured towards a magnificent violet hourglass. Carter stepped forward, peering into the sand as it revealed the moment he'd found the dragon at Happy Tails.

"Why show me this?" Carter whispered. "Because time has meaning," Lowell replied. "Every choice shifts your path. Courage isn't about never falling. It's about trusting you can still fly afterward. Have faith." From his pocket, Lowell produced a round pocket watch, etched with a purple dragon. "This will help you find your way back to yourself. This will help you remember the lessons from the Clock Tower." Carter's hand closed around the watch. A steady warmth pulsed through him. Inside, something wonderful had clicked **Faithfulness**.

Faith to be true to himself. Faith that things would work out. But the golden gears around him slowed, flickering. It was getting dangerously close to the time his wings would disappear.

Carter bolted toward the balcony. He leaped, wings unfurling with a thunderous snap. The flight home was a blur of starlight and shadows. He skimmed rooftops, gliding past a church steeple where the bell chimed softly, almost as if in farewell. He soared over the Whispering Veil River, where the water shimmered silver in the moonlight, and past the park where the swings rocked gently in the night breeze, as if invisible children played there still.

Carter pressed a hand against his pocket where the watch glowed faintly, a heartbeat against his palm. When he reached his street, a ripple of unease spread through him. Something was wrong. All the downstairs lights were on. Not just the kitchen. The living room, the hallway, even the porch light, blazed like a spotlight.

"Carter…" His parents were calling him. Luckily for Carter, his wings had retracted, and he looked like himself. Holding his breath, he opened the creaking door and hesitantly descended the stairs. He didn't know what was waiting for him, but it was time to find out.

Was this another test of his Faith? He stepped into the doorway slowly, heart racing, and saw both his parents at the dining table. His mom looked concerned. His dad had a crumpled paper in his hand. "Carter," his mom said gently, "We found this." Carter's eyes widened. It was one of his journal pages, the one he'd written about Armi, the lake, and the night he had saved her. "We didn't know you were feeling all of this," his dad added, softer now. "Flying or not, these words are powerful. You're brave, Carter. And we're proud of the way you think and care."Carter blinked. He wasn't in trouble for flying. He wasn't caught sneaking out. He was caught… being honest. Being vulnerable. He nodded slowly, unsure what to say.

Then his mom pushed a mug of cocoa toward him and said, "We just want to know more. Can you tell us? About everything?"

Carter sat down. The dragon's glow, tucked in his pocket, warmed his side like a quiet nod. He wasn't alone. And he was finally ready to tell the truth without revealing the lotion or the wings, but about a dream. "It's just something I imagined," he began. "A dream that felt so real, I had to write it down. The lake, the flying, the people I helped… they were part of it. Maybe not real in the way you think, but real enough to mean something."

His parents exchanged a glance, the concern in their eyes softening. "We're glad you dreamed of something so brave and beautiful," his mom said. "And that you shared it."

Carter smiled, just a little. The kind of smile that says maybe everything really will be okay. His Faith was cemented. But as he sipped the coca, warm and sweet against his tongue, he caught something out of the corner of his eye. His parents exchanged another glance—one that lasted just a little too long. His mom's gaze lingered on his pocket, where the dragon's glow pulsed faintly through the fabric before fading away. They didn't say anything. Not yet. Carter's heart skipped a beat, but he forced himself to breathe. Maybe they thought it was just the firelight. Maybe they didn't see it at all. Or maybe… they knew more than they were letting on.

Carter's heart still thudded as he climbed the stairs later that night, the cocoa still warm in his stomach but not quieting the questions in his head. His parents hadn't pressed him, but their glance… it hadn't left him. And the glow in his pocket? It hadn't dimmed until he was alone in his room again.

Lying in bed, Carter traced the scales on the dragon jar through the silk cloth. For the first time, he wondered if his parents already knew something—maybe not about the lotion, maybe not about the wings, but about him. That thought didn't scare him. It steadied him. Because if they saw more than he realized…maybe that was part of **Faithfulness** too. Trusting that even when the truth flickered at the edges, he wasn't entirely on his own. The dragon jar pulsed softly in his hands. The wings inside him stirred. And Carter knew the next adventure was already calling.

Library of Whispers

It took over a week for Carter to absorb all that had happened. He was growing wise beyond his years with some of the experiences and freedom the magical dragon had given him. He was finding himself more open and brave. So far, he has found Joy, Love, Gentleness, and Faithfulness. Feeling stronger with each lesson, excited for the next gift.

There was something shifting inside him, a calmness that wasn't there before. He didn't just feel magical. He felt purposeful. When the dragon glowed again, it wasn't sudden or shocking. It was quiet. Confident like a lantern lighting the way instead of a firework exploding. Lotion applied again, the sensation of the wings fully expanding. Neil stood at his bedroom window, the cool air brushing his cheeks.

He didn't hesitate this time. He leaped from the second-story window, letting the air fill his magnificent wings and lift him into the night. There was a change in Carter, and he felt the wings guiding him, not pulling or pushing, but inviting. The stars winked at him like old friends meeting at the park. Down below, the city of Hollow Creek dozed. Carter approached an old building that seemed familiar, but from his new perspective, he couldn't quite place why that was. The wings guided him to the rooftop of the old brick building, and Carter initiated his graceful landing. Whatever was waiting tonight… he was ready.

The Dragon of Happy Tails

The top of the building had a large open skylight, which Carter felt drawn to and wanted to inspect. Once Carter peered into the skylight, he saw large wooden structures. With a gentle leap, Carter tucked his wings and began his descent. An overwhelming smell of old pages, leather, coffee, dust, and a little bit of

cinnamon. While nearing his destination, the floor, bookshelves towered like enchanted trees in a paper forest. Moonlight poured in through tall windows, spilling across the marble floors like liquid silver. Shadows moved, but not from anything frightening. They drifted like whispers, soft and knowing.

The library was awake. Bookshelves loomed like enchanted trees in a paper forest. Shadows didn't lurk; they whispered, soft and knowing. Then the books themselves stirred. Pages flipped without hands. Covers yawned open. Words peeled off like sparks, floating upward—glowing letters, fluttering like fireflies or butterflies spun from ink. They giggled, danced, and dissolved. A globe in the corner spun slowly, glowing blue. Empires rose and crumbled in time-lapse across their surface, kingdoms folding and fading like paper castles.

Carter's jaw dropped. "Okay. My library card definitely doesn't cover this."

"Welcome back, Carter Jamyson," a voice said gently behind him. He turned. It wasn't Ms. Derkin, the librarian with her chunky necklaces and jokes about overdue books. No, this librarian was stitched from something otherworldly. Her coat was patchwork paper—folded origami pages sewn into flowing sleeves. Her eyes twinkled like starlight through a telescope. Her smile was so kind it felt like an invitation to breathe.

"I... I've never been here at night," Carter stammered, his voice small in the cavernous silence, feeling the weight of wonder settle in his chest.

"You have now," she said, eyes alight. "My name is Paige Turner. You can just call me Ms. Paige. Here, every question is worth asking. Even the ones you're afraid to say out loud." Carter wandered among shelves that stretched far past the building's walls. Some books glowed faintly.

He reached forward, and a book from the shelf took flight, flapping its cover like a bird, gently landing open in his hand. When Carter admired the book, it exploded with life. Gasping as images became animated—he was watching the dreams of great inventors: Da Vinci sketching flying machines in candlelight; Nikola Tesla staring at lightning like it was music; Mae Jemison spinning in space, dancing with the stars.

He opened another book and heard a lion cub's first roar, raw and triumphant, echoing through the savanna bathed in dawns and morning light. As quickly as it came, the book took flight again, leading Carter to a wall of bookshelves.

As Carter approached the wall of bookshelves, he felt the ground start to rumble. The wings Carter wore on his back appeared to be instructing the shelves to separate. The immovable wall of shelves and books opened outward, leading to a secret room filled with lit candles burning with a blue flame. In the center of the room was a weathered stone desk holding a single book. Carter felt compelled to open it. The book was deep brown and leather-bound, with strange inscriptions pressed into the cover. Carter placed both his hands on the ancient book and felt a strong pulse through his body, causing him to wince in pain. Once Carter opened his eyes, the strange writing became clear, and he could understand.

"The gift that was given, what will you choose?"

It felt like the book had been written just for him. "Books don't just tell you who someone else is," the librarian said, appearing beside him once more. "They help you discover who you are. They remind you that your voice matters, even when it's quiet. Especially when it's quiet." Carter stood still, the magic wrapping around him like his favorite blanket. He felt something shifting inside, not a loud change, but a steady one. Like a lantern being lit in a dark room. A loud, distinct sound of a clock striking midnight was deep and resonant, each chime echoing with a clear, solemn tone. The initial strike cut through the stillness, followed by evenly spaced, lingering reverberations.

As the count progressed, the metallic clang grew rhythmically familiar, each note fading slightly before the next begins, filling the silence with a steady, compelling cadence until the final, fading chime leaves the air quiet once more. Carter had to begin his return flight home.

Library of Whispers

He took his powerful wings, forcing the air beneath him, and floated through the skylight. The library began to sing its farewell with a soft rustling of pages. He looked back one more time. The words that had danced in the air now shimmered above the entrance:

"Your story is waiting. Write it with wonder."

Carter soared home under the starlit sky, his heart glowing with possibility. For the first time, he didn't just feel like a boy with wings, he felt like a boy with purpose. A boy whose story was just beginning.

As Carter entered his room and softly lay on his bed, he began to read the ancient book. The book pages contain the strange markings that only Carter had the ability to read. As he read the book, the pages became blurry and slowly faded to black. Carter finally felt true peace and fell fast asleep.

The Colosseum in the Sky

Waking up in his room, a little disoriented, breathing heavily, Carter begins to examine the room. Everything appeared to be where it was supposed to be; however, there was no sign of his book. Carter thought to himself, "I guess last night really was a dream." Carter took both his hands to rub his eyes, THUNK! "OUCH," whimpered Carter. Upon further evaluation, he noticed the ancient book was in his right hand, which smacked him in the face. Carter yelled out loud, "Last night was real!" He got dressed, ready to embrace the day. Swinging his door open wide, he came face to face with an oh-so familiar smell. He slipped down the stairs. When he reached the dining room, there were mounds of food perched on the table. Since he was feeling famished, he dug right in. Waffles, bacon, sausage, and strawberry jam with toast went down the hatch without discrimination. Carter was ready to tackle the day. He could hear the faint hum of a lawnmower outside, reminding him of his chores yet to be tackled. Carter's thoughts were miles above all that, already soaring somewhere between clouds and constellations.

 Carter needed to regroup and finish his weekend list — dishes, check; yard work, check; pretending not to be impatient, double check — the waiting was unbearable. The sun crawled across the sky like it knew he was waiting for night to fall.

 Dinner was another lively family feast, full of clinking silverware and stories that blurred together as Carter's mind drifted elsewhere. He finished his plate in record time, mumbling a quick "' Excuse me!" before darting to his room.

He flopped onto his bed, intending to wait just a few minutes for the stars to come out, but the warmth of his blankets and the hum of the evening lulled him into a deep, unexpected sleep.

Then—FLASH.

A sharp burst of silvery light spilled across his room, slicing through the darkness like moonlight in a dream. Carter blinked awake, heart pounding, the glow painting his walls with swirling reflections. For a second, he didn't remember where he was. Then it hit him — the mission.

Tonight wasn't for sleeping. Tonight was for flying.

Carter leaped from bed, adrenaline sparking through him like electricity, ready to test just how far his wings could carry him. Carter meticulously prepared himself for the journey that awaited him, grabbing his glass dragon and putting on an old sweatshirt, then he cut slits where his wings would sprout. Determination was smeared all over his face, and he began to apply the magical lotion to his shoulders under his sweatshirt. Bright light filled every crevice in the room, but Carter was determined and prepared. Eyes wide open, Carter witnessed radiant streams of light circling the room and felt every fiber of his being change. This time it was different.

Carter noticed the ground began to fall further away, and he felt much heavier; his wings began to grow. Admiring the differences, it was astounding. He had gained at least twenty pounds and grew about a foot, which explains his hunger. His wings were also significantly bigger. Then, whoosh, his wings cast glimmers of moonlight with every gentle flap. With one deep breath and a running leap from his bedroom window, Carter shot into the sky like a comet. Each experience with the potion became easier and more second nature as it became a part of his true nature.

Hollow Creek glittered beneath him, its lights like fireflies caught in a jar. However high above the clouds, there was a Colosseum bustling with excitement and anticipation, like an unfinished story. The field's massive oval yard yawned open in the darkness, and the scoreboard stood silent like a sleeping giant. The lights were off, but the moon had clocked in for duty, casting a silver spotlight right across the 50-yard line. Carter thought to himself, "Wings will help me fly to heights that I have never reached before."

Not from a glowing dragon or a whispering clock tower. This one came from inside his own chest from the place where butterflies live and old gym class memories hang around like stubborn shadows. He wanted to fly over the Hollow Creek football field. Although what he encountered was more like a Colosseum, much grander and magical, it floated high above the clouds.

This place was magical and had all sorts of mystical creatures. There were people as spectators, all of Carter's friends and classmates. They were not able to participate in the events. But they were there to witness the righting of the game where Carter fumbled a pass so badly that the team lost the game point. The memory had clung to him like static ever since. But tonight, he wasn't there to fix it. He just wanted to face it with wings, confidence, and self control.

Carter hovered high above the turf, heart pounding. He didn't expect anything magical to happen. But when you're flying with lotion-powered dragon wings, you learn not to underestimate the night. The air was cooling, which was a blessing considering the excitement of what was yet to come. His body was heating up with anticipation.

Suddenly, the field below came alive, shimmering from the moonlight, in a memory soaked with pain and disappointment, goosebumps making their way up and down his body. The turf rippled like water, and ghostly echoes of past games began to rise. Enthusiastic players dashed across the field, cleats soundless on the grass. Coaches paced the sidelines with clipboards made of mist. The stands filled with engaging fans laughing, cheering, stomping feet that made no sound but filled the air with excitement.

Then came the voice. Booming from the announcer's box like a trumpet of triumph:

"And now, taking the field, our surprise guest: Carter Jamyson!"

Carter's jaw dropped. The crowd erupted into applause, roaring like a tidal wave of belief. This time, he could hear the crowd, playing off their enthusiasm, he dove into a barrel roll, looped around the stadium lights, and flew around the goal posts like a dragon-powered stunt pilot. Laughter burst out of him, a full body, belly laugh that made his stomach muscles ache.

He hadn't realized how heavy the memory of that game had been until it was lifted by flight and cheers.

Below, the players formed two lines across the field, shoulder to shoulder. They clapped in rhythm, inviting him down. As Carter dipped lower, he saw their faces, not just football stars, but kids like him. Some looked like dreamers. Others looked like second chances. All of them were smiling. Taking their positions on the field. Excitement growing.

The ball was in play. Carter headed downfield as quickly as he could. The ball was being passed to him. This time, he didn't fumble. He caught the ball and swiftly dashed between the other players, narrowly avoiding grabs and tackles. As Carter quickly advanced towards the goal post, two opponents, large in stature, began quickly closing the distance from his right rear side. Fully absorbing the totality of the circumstances, Carter scanned his left flank. He made a lateral pass to one of the boys, who wore a face that looked like he needed a second chance.

With great speed, tenacity, and agility, the young man burst through the remainder of the field and entered the end zone. The entirety of the crowd stood to their feet, releasing a roar of cheers that shook the entire stadium. As the crowd went wild, the boy who had just scored, his eyes had changed, no longer needing a second chance, now with eyes full of hope. A wrong from the past was righted. Carter was not only redeemed, but he was a part of a team making it happen together, which was more satisfying than taking all of the glory for himself.

One player leaped up and gave him a high-five, mid-air, his palm glowing briefly with golden sparks. Another cupped his hands around his mouth and shouted, "Keep flying, kid!" Carter's grin was so wide it felt like it reached his ears.

He dipped lower still, soaring through the tunnel of cheering players, his wings catching tiny bursts of wind from every joyful clap. It felt like being part of something huge. Not just a game but a celebration of everyone who had ever tried again, after failing. For the first time, that old game moment didn't sting. It shimmered. Like the metal that was placed around his neck. A reminder of sweet victory. It wasn't erased. It was rewritten. Not with perfection. But with pride.

As Carter rose into the night sky once more, the stadium lights winked on for just a second, just long enough to see his shadow stretch triumphantly across the field. And in that moment, Carter understood something deep in his bones: Bravery doesn't mean never fumbling. It means showing up again, anyway. It means flying straight over the place you once fell and waving. It means believing you are more than your mistakes. He realized he had developed self-control. As he glided home, Hollow Creek glowing below him, Carter felt lighter than air. Not because of the wings. But because of something inside him that had finally let go. And somewhere, faintly, as he soared through the stars......the crowd kept cheering.

It was a night to remember, forever a part of his soul...

Falls of kindness

Carter hadn't used the magic lotion in a couple of weeks. Not because he'd lost it or forgotten about it. The jar still sat on his shelf, nestled between a flashlight with half-dead batteries and the rubber dinosaur missing a tail. The dragon, etched in swirling glass, shimmered with its usual glow. But he just… didn't reach for it. Maybe it was a test. Maybe he wanted to know if he was still brave without wings. Or maybe just maybe he needed to feel what it meant to miss the magic. But one evening, as moonlight streamed through his window like soft silver ribbons, Carter sat cross-legged on his bed, staring at the little dragon. A strange thought tickled the back of his mind, quieter than a whisper but impossible to ignore.

Pondering all that had happened, all that he had experienced, was he ready to fly again? What would he do when the magic ran out? Would he feel different? He would always remember, or would the memories fade? Only time would tell.

After much consideration, he once again reached for the dragon and compressed the magic button. The potion was glowing baby blue this time. Strange, Carter thought. He still trusted the process of the potion; it was enchanted, obviously. Knowingly, he applied it to his shoulders and felt the warmth and power envelop him. He would never tire of this feeling. Glorious sparkling scales brightened his room. Carter was ready.

Perched on the windowsill, Carter's wings glowed softly under the light of the moon as he soared beyond his usual nighttime route. Tonight, he was just flying aimlessly. A quiet tug in his chest guided him north, past the city limits, over forests, rivers, and sleeping towns.

Soon, he heard it: a roar like thunder, steady and wild. Water rushing with power and speed, enough current to power an entire city. Then he saw it.

Niagara Falls.

Lit up like a rainbow. With different colors. A wondrous sight so brilliant it's hard to describe. He hovered above the cascading water, mist curling up around him like breath from a giant. The sound was deafening, yet peaceful, like the earth singing.

Carter spotted a hidden ledge tucked behind the roaring wall of water — a pocket of mist and moonlight that shimmered like a secret. He glided toward it, wings scattering droplets that sparkled around him like tiny diamonds. There, sitting on the stone ledge, legs dangling, was a boy. He looked about twelve, maybe two years older than Carter, with sharp features and restless energy. His sneakers were scuffed, his jeans were soaked, and his ball cap was pulled low over his brow. But when he looked up, Carter caught the flash of stormy brown eyes — eyes that had seen too much and trusted too little.

"Whoa," the boy said, blinking hard. "You've got wings."

Carter grinned, landing beside him. "Yep. Magic wings I grow them when someone needs me or I need to learn who I am from places I go and people I meet."

The boy snorted. "I'm Kai," he muttered, glancing back at the waterfall. "You're not from around here, huh?"

"You could say that," Carter said, folding his wings carefully. "What about you?"

Kai shrugged, his voice almost lost in the thunder of the falls. "I ran away. Again." He kicked a loose pebble over the edge and watched it vanish into the mist. "I don't belong where they put me. The group home. They say I'm a handful." His tone dripped with sarcasm, but there was something small and scary under it.

Falls of kindness

Carter was quiet for a moment, letting the roar of the water fill the space between them. The colors of the falls shifted green, gold, violet, and blue — reflecting in Kai's eyes like pieces of some bigger truth neither of them could name.

"That doesn't sound like a handful," Carter said softly. "That sounds like a heart that hasn't been heard."

Kai froze. For a second, his tough expression cracked. "That's... weirdly nice," he said. "You practice that or something?" Carter laughed. "Nope. Comes free with the wings."

They sat in silence for a while, watching the lights shimmer through the waterfall. The air was heavy with mist, cool and clean, and for once, Kai didn't look like he wanted to run. He looked like a kid who finally found somewhere he could breathe.

Carter reached into his pocket and pulled out a folded scrap of paper — a little wrinkled, soft from being held too often. "Here," he said, handing it to Kai. "It's a map. My kind of map. It doesn't show places. It shows people, the ones worth finding... and the ones worth being."

Kai frowned but took it. When he unfolded it, the mist around them glowed faintly. At the center of the page, written in shimmering gold ink, were the words:

"You are not forgotten."

Kai's lip trembled, his eyes tearing up, and he quickly blinked it away. "You're weird," he muttered, but his voice was smaller now, less guarded.

Carter smiled. "Yeah. But sometimes the weird ones fly the highest."

Kai huffed a small laugh, shaking his head. "You really believe that?" Carter spread his wings slightly, scales glinting like moonlit armor.

"Every night." For a long moment, the thunder of the falls was all that existed — and then, in the misty glow, Kai dug into his hoodie pocket and pulled out a small silver coin on a string. He slipped it out and pressed it into Carter's hand. "My mom gave me this before... before things got hard," Kai said quietly. "She said it was for luck. I think you probably need it more than I."

Carter looked down at the coin, already glowing faintly silver in his palm.

"Thanks," he said, voice soft. "But maybe it works both ways."

The air shimmered around them, and Carter felt warmth bloom in his chest. Light pulsed through the coin, brightening until it transformed into something new, two golden medallions stamped with the word **Kindness**.

The coins hummed softly in his hand, like a heartbeat that didn't belong to just one person. He looked up, but Kai was staring at it, also wide-eyed. "Guess it still works," Kai said with a shaky smile.

Carter nodded. "Because you shared it. Look, it grew into two. Now we can each have one to remember, this night that our friendship was formed."

The mist swirled again, catching the moonlight, and Carter knew it was time to go. He stood, wings extended in a glittering arc of scales and feathers. The spray from the falls painted his wings in rainbows as he turned back to Kai. "Don't forget what's on that map," Carter said. "You're on it, too. I will always be your friend." After they exchanged numbers, Kai remained on the ledge, the map glowing softly in his hands.

Kai nodded, clutching the paper like it was a treasure as well as the friendship medallion. "Don't crash into anything. I will see you again someday," he called after him. And in the heart of the storm, the word **Kindness** echoed between two boys, one mastering the flight, the other remembering how to hope. The spray from the falls caught the moonlight, scattering tiny prisms that looked like a thousand miniature rainbows bursting into the night. Carter couldn't help but laugh as he leaped into the sky. The mist chased him upward, above the glowing waters, the falls roaring their farewell.

The flight home felt different this time. Lighter. Not because the journey was shorter, it wasn't, but because Carter's heart carried something new. The steady coin of Kindness rested in his pocket, warm against his side, almost like a heartbeat that didn't belong to him alone.

Below, the cities and towns passed quietly, their lights blinking softly in the distance. He traced the familiar bends of the Whispering Veil River, the silver ribbon guiding him toward Hollow Creek. He flew lower as his neighborhood came into view, roofs lined like toy blocks, the streetlamps humming like sleepy guardians.

When he finally landed on his windowsill, the house was still and dark.

No glowing lights. No waiting voices. Just the comfort of home. He tucked his wings away, slipped inside, and placed the coin gently beside his other treasures-the rock from the zoo, the glowing obs, the pocket watch, the magical book.

Carter whispered quietly, "**Kindness** is hearing someone when the world goes quiet around them."

And for the first time, the word didn't feel small at all. He slid beneath his covers, heart still humming with the roar of Niagara, and drifted into sleep. Tomorrow will come. And with it, another dream, another flight, another lesson. But tonight, he rested, knowing that flight was never just about the wings. It was about what he carried back with him.

That night, kindness didn't feel small. It felt like Niagara Falls sounds, steady and unshakable, like a thunder that never quits. The closer you get, the more it wraps around you, filling your chest, impossible to ignore. Wild, real, and bigger than words, a symphony of nature's force.

The Carnival at the Carousel

Carter's wings shimmered as he followed a breeze that didn't quite feel like air; it felt like music.

A melody, soft at first, like a violin warming up, then building into a playful tune that tugged at his heart. It carried him north through the twilight skies, guiding him like invisible sheet music written across the stars. Below, glowing lights began to gather near the bend of a sleepy river town. Neil drifted lower and gasped. There, in a circle of mist, stood a carousel. Not just any carousel, it was the kind with chipped paint that somehow made it more beautiful, frozen in time. Its brass poles gleamed faintly in the moonlight, the kind of glow that belonged to memory. And the creatures? Not horses at all, but dragons and mythical beasts frozen mid-flight, their carved wings tucked close, scales dulled with age.

The closer he got, the more vibrant the details became. The paint was blooming back into color, tarnish turning to gleam, wood seams laminated smoothly together as if time itself were running backward.

Then the smell hit him.

Roasted peanuts. Cotton candy. Popcorn.

Carter's stomach growled. His heart did a double flip. "No way," he whispered. "It smells like a carnival!" He landed softly beside a pole shaped like a dragon's tail, sneakers making the faintest thud. The moment his feet touched the platform, the carousel shuddered. One by one, the lights blinked on—first a single bulb, then another, then a hundred more until the whole ride blazed like a crown of stars.

The air filled with music: a calliope's song bursting into life, jaunty and lilting, pulling him into its rhythm. The dragons began to move—first a slow sway, then a lively prance. Their scales caught the starlight and reflected it back like dancing flames. But it wasn't just the ride that came alive.

From the carousel's spin, a carnival began to bloom. Red-and gold tents sprang from the mist, lanterns floated into the air, and a Ferris wheel unfolded like a silver flower in fast motion. Fireflies spelled glowing words in the sky, "Welcome! and Shine Bright!" before swirling into constellations. The once-empty field had transformed into a festive carnival, alive with laughter, light, and the hum of magic that felt older than the stars.

And the people-oh, the people! They shimmered faintly, as if made from the same light that glowed beneath Carter's wings. Their laughter sparkled, their joy contagious. Carter's heart swelled; he'd never seen anything so impossibly vibrant. He wandered first to **Miss Clementine's Candy Apple Stall**, where the air shimmered with sugar and cinnamon. Miss Clementine had kind eyes, an apron sprinkled with sugar crystals, and a voice like warm honey. "You've got the look of someone who brings light with 'em," she said, handing him a caramel apple without asking for a ticket.

Carter took a bite, crunch, and for a second, the sweetness seemed to flow through him, filling his veins with courage. "Wow," he said, wide-eyed. "That's the best thing I've ever tasted."

Miss Clementine winked. "Magic knows how to find the ones who need it most."

Next came **Jack-Hoon the Juggler**, a boy about Carter's age, with hair like spun bronze and a grin that dared you to join the fun; it was contagious. He was balancing twelve bowling pins while whistling a tune that matched the carousel's melody. When he spotted Carter, he tossed one pin in his direction. "Hey, winged boy! Think fast!" Carter yelped, caught it clumsily, and nearly dropped it. Jack laughed so hard he had to catch two more pins mid-fall. "Not bad for a first try! Want to learn?"

Carter hesitated. "I'm not that good at stuff like this."

Jack shrugged, handing him three pins. "Goodness starts with trying." Carter tried. He wobbled, fumbled, dropped one, caught another, and nearly took out a cotton candy stand, but Jack cheered louder than anyone. "See? You're getting it! It's not about being perfect. It's about the **Joy** in trying."

Carter laughed, cheeks warm, feeling that same melody tugging at his heart again, like the air itself was applauding. At the duck pond game, he met a five-year-old girl named Addalyn with wild, dark, blonde, wavy hair pulled into two braids, big blue eyes, and pink overalls. She sighed as she picked up duck, after duck, finding no stars beneath them. "No luck?" Carter asked. She shook her head, looking ready to give up. Carter smiled when he picked up a winning duck gold star and all. He handed it to her with a grin. "Here. I think this one's yours." Her whole face lit up like a sparkler on the 4th of July.

"Thank you!" she squealed, hugging her prize, a giant stuffed rabbit, tight. "You're like a hero from a storybook!"

Carter laughed. "Nah. Just someone who really likes carnival games." Addalyn giggled and skipped away, but Carter noticed something strange: Her footsteps left trails of light that slowly faded, like fireflies drifting into the stars.

Carter followed the light trail to the center of the fair. There stood a glowing ticket booth. Inside, a man with a beard, as white and fluffy as whipped cream, leaned forward. His eyes twinkled in a way that made Carter's heart ache. It reminded him of Grandpa; he was missing him in a big way, the way he used to smile over card games and fishing. He missed his younger years, when he lived near his grandparents. Now that he was getting older, he cherished the times they had together even more.

"You've got a strong heart," the man said gently, sliding open the booth window. "Sometimes the greatest power isn't flying. It's choosing to do good when no one's watching."

He reached beneath the counter and pulled out a tiny velvet box no bigger than a marshmallow and a golden ticket. He placed them in Carter's hands. "A reminder," he said. Carter opened the tiny velvet box slowly. Nestled inside was a golden carousel pin, shaped like a dragon mid-flight. As Neil turned it over, a word shimmered in the air above it, drifting like a glowing cloud: **Goodness.**

Carter swallowed hard, tucking the pin into his pouch beside Kindness and Gentleness. The pouch was getting heavier not with weight, but with meaning. He thanked the bearded man, then asked what the golden ticket was for. The old man said, "You'll need it to enter the race. Good luck, son." Perplexed, Carter asked, "What race?" Then came the voice. Deep and warm. "Looks like the dragons are waking up." Carter turned to see a thin boy with brown hair, kind brown eyes, and huge dimples when he smiled. He was wearing a shimmering red ringmaster's coat, his eyes full of mischief and starlight. "Care for a race, young flyer? I'm Ringmaster Deacon. I see you have the potential to slay dragons. Step right up and join the race."

Before Deacon could answer, the carousel slowed, and the creatures were lowering their heads as if bowing to him. Carter ran to the one that had caught his eye from the start: silver-scaled, fierce yet kind, with markings like lightning bolts down its neck. The dragon, with emerald green and sapphire eyes, leaned closer. The plaque hanging from his neck read "Granger". Instincts kicking in, Carter knew Granger was his Steed; the connection was undeniable. Carter climbed on. Handing his golden ticket to Ringmaster Deacon, ready for the race.

The wood beneath him trembled, paint flaking away, revealing living scales beneath. The dragon blinked. Its wings extended with a rush of wind and light. The carousel started to spin. Then it spun faster, music building to a fever pitch. The whole carousel came to life. And then—Boom! The carnival erupted in cheers as a glowing race track unfolded before them, stretching through the sky like a ribbon of starlight.

The creatures lined up, wings flexed, tails coiling, their voices magnified, with roars, with the excitement and anticipation of the race. The ringmaster raised his cane, and with a flash of gold sparks, illuminated the starting line.

Deacon shouted, **"Fly!"**

Carter's dragon leaped forward, the wind howling in his ears, laughter bubbling from his chest. The dragons, griffins, phoenixes, unicorns, and serpents with jeweled eyes all blazed along, jockeying for first place.

They dove and climbed, twirled through rings of light, weaving past comets of fireworks that burst like stars reborn. All magnificent and strong, each with its own strength. Carter leaned forward, whispering, "We've got this." Carter extended his wings to give the extra boost needed to pass the serpent, which was in the lead. The dragon roared, wings slicing through the final gate in a burst of emerald fire. Deacon declared with excitement "Ladies, gentlemen, and dreamers of every realm — behold your champion of the skies, the swift and the fearless… Carter of Hollow Creek!"

The crowd exploded in applause. The dark sky lit by fireworks spelling Victory! Carter threw up his hands and laughed. "We did it!" Then Granger turned his great head, eyes gleaming, and rumbled a soft, satisfied purr. "You flew true," a voice seemed to whisper in Carter's mind. As dawn's first light crept across the horizon, the carnival began to fade, music softening, lanterns dimming, dragons folding their wings. Carter dismounted, his hand lingering on the dragon's warm scales. "Thank you," he whispered. The dragon blinked once, then bowed its head before turning back into polished wood, in his place, on the carousel.

The carnival was folding inward like closing petals of a flower. Carter's vision swirled, colors melting into dawn. The carousel stilled, but the air shimmered with quiet magic. Carter stood alone in the empty field, just himself and the carousel in the morning breeze, cool against his face. He glanced at his reflection in one of the brass poles and saw a faint sparkle of a few stars still glowing in the sky. He needed to hustle to beat the sunrise. He smiled. "I'll see you again," he said softly.

Then, with one smooth motion of his wings, he took off toward the rising sun, leaving behind the carnival that might just be waiting for the next dreamer to find it. He blinked — and found himself back in his room.

The Dragon of Happy Tails

Morning light spilled through the curtains. Birds chirped. His heart was still pounding. For a second, he wondered if it had all been a dream. Then something moved at the foot of his bed.

Granger, smaller now, no bigger than a kitten, lay curled up, scales glinting faintly. A wisp of silver smoke curled from his tiny nostrils. Carter gaped. "You're... real?" The dragon yawned, stretched, and looked at him with lazy, golden eyes. Around its neck hung a golden ticket, embossed with a carousel and flying dragons and other mystical creatures. Carter picked it up and read the words engraved across it:

ONE RIDE ANYTIME — THE CARNIVAL AWAITS.

His eyes widened, a grin spreading across his face. "You're staying?" Granger gave a tiny huff of approval and snuggled deeper into the blanket.

Just then, a knock came at the door. "Carter? You awake, honey?" his mom called.

Carter panicked. "Uh..just getting dressed!" he said quickly, shoving the small dragon under his pillow. A tiny puff of smoke rose from beneath it. "Shhh!" Carter whispered. The dragon's tail flicked, accidentally setting off a spark that singed the corner of Carter's comic book. Carter waved the smoke away frantically. "No, no, no-quiet! You're supposed to be mythical, not mischievous!"

"Is everything okay in there?" his mom asked.

"Yep! Totally fine! Definitely not hiding a dragon!" he blurted before realizing what he was saying. Silence.

Then, she said, "What?" "Nothing! Love you!" he said, grinning nervously as her footsteps faded. Carter lifted the pillow. Granger looked up innocently, a puff of silver smoke forming the shape of a heart.

Carter laughed softly. "You're trouble." Granger blinked, curling back up with a contented sigh. Carter picked up the golden ticket again and whispered, "Guess we're in this together." As Carter lay back, the tiny dragon's tail curled around his wrist like a friendship bracelet made of light. Outside, he could hear the faint melody of calliope music drifting on the breeze, playful and bright, promising more adventures to come.

The carnival wasn't gone.

It was waiting.

The Mansion of Forgotten Echoes

Carter tilted the dragon jar beneath the moonlight. The shimmering silver lotion wasn't gone, but it was thinner than before, like clouds stretched across too much sky. It clung lazily to the bottom, glowing faintly, as if saving its best for something important. Carter dipped his fingers in carefully, rubbing the cool magic across his shoulders, slower this time. Reverently.

His wings whispered to life with a soft shhhh, like pages turning in a forgotten library book. They didn't roar tonight. Instead, they glowed gently, with the steady calm of something ancient and sure. Carter stepped onto his window ledge, took a deep breath, and lifted into the sky. Carter kept Grange tucked under his hoodie most nights now. His parents thought he'd rescued a stray lizard from the park, and he wasn't about to correct them.

The stars above, Hollow Creek, blinked their sleepy approval as he soared past them, higher and higher, until the city's lights stretched into a glittering quilt below. But tonight felt different. Not because the jar was running low, though it was. No, this felt like… a turning page like a story waiting for its next, most important chapter.

His wings guided him past the Hollow Creek Art Museum, where he'd love to explore. Not tonight, for tonight it was guiding him somewhere older. As they neared the mansion, Grange squirmed on his shoulder, his glassy scales glowing faintly blue. It wasn't random; he was guiding Carter, tugging him toward the gates like he recognized something in the shadows ahead.

"Easy, buddy," Carter whispered. "You've been here before, huh?" The dragon gave a soft hum that buzzed through Carter's collarbone. It wasn't just curiosity; it was a memory. Grange belonged to places like this, where forgotten dreams waited to be found again.

Carter smiled. Maybe that's why Grange had found him.

A place he half remembered from a third-grade field trip: the grand, mysterious, and slightly spooky Waverly Hollow Hall & Gardens. Back then, it had felt too big, too old, too full of secrets. Even now, under the moonlight, the mansion looked like a giant stone riddle, whispering into the woods. Chimneys pointed skyward like watchful guards. Ivy curled tightly around the windows, as though the house was trying to keep its memories from escaping. Carter drifted toward a vine-laced balcony, and before his sneakers even touched the railing, the doors creaked open.

"Come on in," said a voice soft and melodic, like wind chimes echoing in a dream. Inside, the hallway stretched forever, lined with suits of armor and enormous tapestries. A chandelier hung above, as massive as a UFO. The air was still... but not silent. Whispers hummed through the corridors, curious, like the mansion was waking up, and he felt the presence of someone. "Who's there?" Carter asked, his voice bouncing down the empty hall. The answer came in flickers of light. Glowing orbs zipped around him like fireflies on parade. One hovered right in front of his nose, giggling in a sound, like glitter.

The orbs darted down a smaller corridor, giggling. Carter followed the giggling orbs, their light guiding him past doors that whispered as he passed. Finally, orbs led him to a glowing staircase and down a long secret hall. In the hall, the orbs stopped in front of one heavy wooden door painted with faded suns and moons — inviting him to discover what would be revealed behind the door.

He pushed on the door; to his surprise, it opened. Carter cautiously entered. Inside was a playroom, huge and full of dust bunnies that danced in the window light like tiny stars. Toys from another century sat in perfect order — wooden trains, stuffed bears, and kites with tails made of ribbons. But at the far end of the room stood a mirror. Tall, rippling like silver water, humming softly. "Welcome back, Winged One."

"Back?" Carter frowned. "I've never, oh wait. I have been here. On a field trip. With my class."

The mirror shimmered, showing not just the boy with wings but every version of him. The shy kid who never raised his hand. The one who doodled dragons in his notebook. The one who climbed, too, high in trees just to test the air. The one who failed. The one who kept trying anyway.

Then the mirror stretched wider. Hundreds of children filled its glow. Kids of every kind. Some with scars. Some with glasses. Some with wheelchairs. Some with dreams too big for their rooms. All of them had wings, different and beautiful. Each one is alive with possibility.

"You're not the only one," said a voice deeper than the orbs. Not just etched in glass anymore. Appearing in the mirror as a reflection was the dragon. Not just silent, but alive. Scaled wings folding gently, eyes warm as firelight. Carter's breath caught. The dragon leaned closer, causing Carter to lean closer to the mirror. In a low voice, something only Carter could hear, the dragon said, "You've given the magic more than you've taken. That is why the magic lotion has lasted so long."

Carter's throat tightened in relief, and awe. He nodded slowly. "So I can keep flying?"

The dragon's smile curved like the crescent moon.

"Not just flying. Becoming who you've always been, letting your light shine bright." The orbs flying around them swirled brighter, their laughter chiming like wind through crystal. The mirror dimmed, folding its visions away until only Carter's reflection remained, a boy with glowing wings, wide eyes, and a heart carrying more than just himself.

Carter stepped backward, wings brushing the dusty rocking horse. With one last look at the dragon, before it vanished in the mirror. After experiencing the mansion that now felt alive with secrets, now revealed.

The Mansion of Forgotten Echoes

He turned and made his way back up the glowing staircase. The balcony doors opened on their own, spilling him into the cool night. He spread his wings and leaped.

Beyond it, the city of Hollow Creek stretched like a quilt stitched with light. Carter pressed a hand to his chest. The warmth of the dragon's words lingered there, steady as a heartbeat: Not just flying. Becoming. Carter's wings carried him away from the Mansion of Forgotten Dreams, the echo of the massive halls still clinging to him like cobwebs. His pouch felt heavier than ever with the tokens he'd collected: kindness, gentleness, goodness, yet the weight in his chest told him his journey wasn't finished. Not yet.

He banked toward home, stars winking overhead. The wind carried him like an old friend. Every flap of his wings felt different tonight, not borrowed, but earned. When his feet finally touched the shingles of his roof, Carter didn't feel tired. He felt whole. He whispered to the night, "I'm not the only one." And above him, the stars seemed to nod in quiet agreement. Even in the quiet, Carter could still hear the gentle voices reminding him: gentleness isn't weakness, it's strength wrapped in peace. Carter slept soundly with peace in his heart and Granger by his side...

The Art of Creativity

The Art of Creativity The following weekend. The lotion shimmered faintly when he rubbed a little more across his shoulders. Not as bright as before. The glow that once burst like fireworks now flickered like the last candle on a birthday cake. "Enough for one more flight," he murmured. "Maybe two."

He let the night winds carry him until a glittery shimmer below caught his eye. The Hollow Creek Art Museum glowed like a crystal lantern in the middle of the city, throwing shards of color across the rooftops. He'd flown past it before, always curious, but tonight something was different. The building itself looked awake. Waiting.

Carter landed softly on the rooftop garden, his sneakers clicking against the stone. The glass walls reflected moonlight in ripples, and then, with a slow creak, like a hinge on a giant book, the doors opened on their own. A quiet invitation. Granger peeked out from Carter's sweatshirt as they stepped into the Gallery of Creativity, his tiny claws tapping lightly against his shoulder. The dragon's scales shimmered like stained glass under the museum lights. Carter swore he felt the same warm hum as before, that pull towards forgotten things waiting to come alive again.

"Yeah, I get it," Carter whispered with a grin. "You like places with a little magic left in the cracks." Inside, the air wasn't empty. It hummed a gentle vibration, like a brush held above a canvas, ready for the first stroke.

Paintings flickered, colors shifted. A Van Gogh sky twisted lazily overhead, stars spinning as if they recognized him. A steel sculpture tilted its shadow toward him, as if to wave hello.

Carter walked deeper, wings brushing softly against the air. Portraits turned their gaze as he passed, not in a creepy way, but like something familiar.

And then he saw it.

An enormous painting of a dragon stretched across an entire wall, emerald scales, golden eyes, wings unfurled in a sky alive with light. Carter's breath caught. "That can't be a coincidence," he whispered. "No such thing as coincidence here," said a voice. Carter spun around. Out from behind a sculpture of a bird stepped a girl about his age. She wore paint-splattered overalls and had a messy bun that barely contained her halo of curls. She held a glowing paintbrush that shimmered with living color.

"I'm Brynn," she said with a grin. "You're the boy who's been collecting the fruits of the spirit, right?"

Carter blinked. "You… know about that?" Brynn twirled her brush, and with one flick, colors poured into the air like liquid light. "I know about imagination," she said. "Same thing, just louder."

He laughed. "You work here?"

"Not work," she said, dipping the brush into thin air again. "Belong. This place holds every bit of creativity kids ever lose, all the drawings, doodles, and dreams too wild for the world outside. Tonight, you were invited into my world." Before Carter could answer, she swept her brush through space, and wings appeared. Wings made of starlight, music, and impossible shapes. They pulsed with the rhythm of laughter itself.

Carter's own wings shimmered in response. "That's… incredible." Brynn smiled. "Creativity is just belief with extra glitter." They wandered the glowing galleries together. Canvases shifted with Carter's thoughts: when he remembered Kai at the Falls, water thundered in a frame; when he thought of Armi by the lake, silver ripples shimmered on painted water. Brynn stopped before a large golden-framed mirror. But instead of his reflection, Carter saw himself soaring over mountains, oceans, and skies he didn't recognize.

The Art of Creativity

Other kids flew beside him, carrying their own colors, leaving streaks of light behind.

"So... what does it mean?" Carter asked quietly.

"It means your story doesn't end with you," Brynn said. "Creativity spreads. What you paint with your life inspires others to pick up their brushes too." Brynn tilted her head, studying a half-finished canvas splashed with sunset colors. "Hey, want to paint something with me?" she asked, her eyes bright. "I've got all this space and only one imagination, it's kind of boring."

Carter laughed and took the extra brush she offered. Side by side, they filled the blank space with color—his strokes clumsy at first, hers sure and wild. But as they worked, the shapes started to make sense: wings of light, shadows of stars, something that looked a lot like hope. When they finally stepped back, Brynn smiled and said softly, "Every dream deserves a little color." Neil twirled his brush, and it shimmered, the wooden handle curling and shrinking until it became a tiny artist's palette that fit neatly in his palm. "Guess it's yours now," Brynn said with a wink. "A reminder that you helped finish something that matters."

Then she reached into the air and pulled something small and shimmering from the swirl of color around them. It was a tiny glass vial filled with swirling liquid light. The colors inside danced like miniature galaxies. She pressed it into Carter's hand. "Here," she said softly. "For when you forget how bright you really are."

Carter turned, looking at the light, mesmerized. "What is it?" "Bottled imagination," Brynn said with a wink. "Whenever you're stuck or scared, open it and remember your ideas aren't gone. They're just waiting for you to notice them." He held it close, the vial glowing faintly against his palm.

"Thank you," he said, his voice small but full of wonder and appreciation. Brynn's gaze flicked to his shoulders, where the glow of the lotion pulsed faintly.

"It won't last forever, you know," she said softly. "Every gift has its season."

Carter nodded. "Then I guess I'd better use it well." As he turned to leave, Brynn dipped her brush one last time and painted a trail of color in the air, a path of stars that seemed to hum just for him. He started toward the door, but when he reached it, it wouldn't budge. He tried again. Locked.

The museum lights flickered once, twice. Brynn laughed lightly. "Guess you'll need a little artistic exit." She lifted her brush and drew a doorway on the glass wall. The colors shimmered, forming a swirling oval of pure light. "Hurry," she said, eyes twinkling. "Sunrise doesn't wait for dreamers."

Carter grinned. "Race you!" They said in unison, as they sprinted forward, wings flaring, leaping straight through the painted doorway. It rippled like water, then burst into color as he soared out into the cool, predawn sky. Behind him, Brynn's laughter followed, bright and echoing, like bells in the wind.

Hollow Creek spread below him, every streetlight glowing like a drop of gold paint on a dark canvas. The air felt alive, humming with color. The stars were fading, and the horizon blushed pink and lavender. "Come on, wings," Carter muttered, heart pounding. "Don't fade yet!" He dipped and climbed, the wind rushing past him, wings flashing in the first light of morning. The museum's reflection shimmered below like a memory painted in light. Just as the first sunbeam touched the rooftops, Carter dove toward home, landing clumsily on his windowsill with a soft thud. His wings vanished in a shimmer before the last glow of the lotion faded completely.

He stumbled into bed just as his bedroom door creaked open. "Carter?" his mom's voice called sleepily. "Everything okay?"

"Uh-huh!" he said, pulling the blanket up to his chin. "Just...dreaming." The door closed. Silence returned. Carter exhaled, heart still racing. He reached into his pocket to check the pouch of tokens and froze. There, nestled among them, was the tiny vial of swirling color. Only now... it glowed faintly in the dawn light, and a tiny brushstroke of blue paint streaked across his fingers.

Carter smiled. "So it was real." Outside, the sky flared pink and gold, as if someone up there had taken a paintbrush and added one last masterpiece to the night. And the little vial by his bedside pulsed once, like a heartbeat keeping time with his next adventure.

The New Dream

In his dream, Carter gasped in wonder. It wasn't a jar. It wasn't a carving. It was a real dragon, tall and majestic, with scales that shimmered in shifting colors: turquoise, pearl, and sky-fire gold. Its wings unfurled behind it like sails on a cosmic ship. "You carried the spark," the dragon said gently. "But you weren't alone. You never were."

Carter's voice wobbled. "I thought I was just… a kid with weird lotion." The dragon chuckled, a sound that made the walls hum.

"You were. And that was more than enough." Something warm pressed into Carter's hand. He looked down. A scale not from his own wings, but older, glowing faintly with golden light. It pulsed with comfort. "For when the lotion runs out," the dragon said. "So you remember. You'll still fly. You always could."

Tears welled in Carter's eyes, not sadness, but something bigger. Joy, belief, belonging. It had taken patience to learn, but it had been worth the journey. "So… is this the end?" he whispered.

The dragon leaned close, eyes twinkling. "No, Carter Jamyson. This… is your beginning."

As dawn crept over Hollow Creek, Carter stepped out of the dream-like mansion and lifted into the air. No lotion. No tricks. Just faith. He flew higher than ever before, not with fear, but with fierce joy. He was a boy with wings. A boy with a story. A boy who believed. And that? That was more than enough. The Dragon's Letter The next morning, Carter awoke to find the glass dragon waiting on his desk.

The lotion was gone, its shimmer only a memory. But beside the glass dragon sat Granger. When Carter extended his arm, Granger climbed right up his arm and settled on his shoulder, purring — or something like it — a soft, vibrating hum. Before Carter could say a word, he spotted the folded note resting where the lotion once sat.

The Dragon's Letter

Dear Carter,

You thought my gift was wings. But the wings were only a mirror. They showed you what was already inside you, your courage, your kindness, your faith, and your joy. Every time you leaped into the night, you weren't just flying through the sky. You were learning how to fly through fear, through doubt, and into wonder.

Remember this: you don't need me anymore. The wings may fade, but what you've discovered will not. The fruits you've gathered — love, joy, peace, patience, kindness, goodness, faithfulness, gentleness, and self-control — are treasures no one can take away. And the extras, courage and creativity, were waiting for you all along. Creativity is what turns dreams into stories, and what paints courage, over fear.

What takes a whisper of hope and makes it sing. Your journey is only beginning. Keep looking up. Keep opening your window. Keep believing. Share what you've learned. Teach others to see the magic in themselves. Because the truest flight isn't soaring above the world, it's lifting the world with you.

With all the belief I can hold,

The Dragon of Happy Tails

Carter held the letter against his chest, feeling its truth settle in. Granger nuzzled his neck and sneezed out a tiny spark, which fizzled harmlessly on the bed sheet. Carter laughed, and so did his mom, who happened to peek in just then. "Carter Jamyson, what on earth is that?" she asked, squinting at the golden, tiny kitten-sized creature perched on her son's shoulder.

Carter hesitated. "Um... my pet gecko. Kind of, his name's Granger."

Granger puffed his chest proudly and flicked his tail like he approved of the description.

His mom tilted her head. "Well… I suppose you can keep him, as long as he doesn't breathe fire or chew cords." Carter and Granger exchanged a quick, conspiratorial glance.

"Deal," Carter said quickly. From that moment on, Granger became part of the household. He perched on windowsills like a guardian gargoyle, curled up inside Carter's hoodie pocket during movie night, and had a curious obsession with warm laundry piles. His parents adored "the little guy," never realizing that when the moonlight hit just right, his scales shimmered like stars trapped in gold.

The Journey Home

That night Carter soared once more over Hollow Creek. The air was crisp, brushing his cheeks as his wings carried him higher and higher. The city twinkled beneath him, streetlights glowing like fireflies scattered across velvet. From up here, he could see it all: the quiet zoo, the sleeping library, the faithful clock tower, and the shining roof line of the Hollow Creek Art Museum. He slowed, as he passed it, remembering Brynn's grin, the glow of her paintbrush, and the mural they'd brought to life together — the one that shimmered with stories only they could see.

As the wind whispered past, Neil felt a faint warmth in his pocket. He reached inside and found the tiny palette charm Brynn had given him, its bristles tipped with a fleck of light that refused to fade. He smiled. "Every brushstroke is like a heartbeat," Brynn had said. "Keep painting your story, Carter." The memory warmed him — a reminder that creativity and friendship had become part of his flight too. Every place below him carried a story now.

His Story.

The lotion's shimmer was gone, but Carter didn't need it. He glided easily, letting the wind cradle him, letting the city sing beneath his wings. He thought of the dragon's letter: Kindness is never wasted. Courage carries you farther than you can imagine. For the first time, Carter didn't wonder if he belonged in the sky. He knew. But home was calling, his little house with the high windows, his bed with rumpled sheets, and his notebook waiting for new stories.

The New Dream

With one last sweeping look at the city of secrets and wonders, Carter tilted his wings and began his descent. The streetlights winked, the trees whispered, and the night seemed to guide him home. He landed softly on his window seal, heart steady, wings folding close. Carter slipped back inside, set the glass dragon on his nightstand, next to a snoozing Granger, and whispered, "Thank you." Then, with the quiet satisfaction of a boy who had seen more than he ever dreamed, he curled beneath his blankets. Sleep swept over him like one final flight, gentle, certain, and free.

And outside, the giant dragon glowed faintly in the moonlight, watching, waiting, and keeping its promise. On the windowsill, tiny Grange stirred, his glassy wings twitching as if dreaming too. He blinked once, eyes gleaming gold, and let out a soft, contented puff of smoke that curled into the shape of a heart. Then he tucked his tail beneath him and rested, a guardian of small wonders, keeping watch over the boy who had learned to fly without needing wings.

Somewhere deep in the quiet night, a faint hum filled the air, the sound of forgotten dreams remembering themselves again.

About the Author

I grew up in Walnut, California, until my family moved to the Central Coast when I was twelve. Life wasn't always easy, and growing up in a volatile environment made me grow up fast. By fifteen, I had graduated from high school and jumped straight into hard ranch work caring for horses (both full-sized and miniature), working in nursing homes and hospitals as a CNA (Certified Nursing Assistant), and later serving ten years as a Correctional Officer at Wasco State Prison and the California Men's Colony. Each step taught me resilience, compassion, and a fair share of creative problem-solving. Through it all, I've held tight to the promise of Jeremiah 29:11: *"For I know the plans I have for you, declares the Lord, plans to prosper you and not to harm you, plans to give you hope and a future."*

At nineteen, I married my husband, Chuck. Together, we've built not only homes as a Realtor and Licensed General Building Contractor team, but also a lively family of eleven children and twelve grandchildren who fill our lives with joy, chaos, and laughter. Proverbs 22:6 *"Train up a child in the way he should go: and when he is old, he will not depart from it."*

Somehow, in the middle of all that noise and fun, I still found time to write Neil Ray and the Dragon of Happy Tails, proving that a little imagination (and maybe a lot of coffee) can go a long way. These days, I'm still building, whether it's houses, stories, or memories— and I believe with all my heart that courage, imagination, and faith can carry us through any storm. Joshua 1:9 *"Have I not commanded you? Be strong and courageous. Do not be afraid; do not be discouraged, for the LORD your God will be with you wherever you go"*

And if you ever see me flying by with a mug of cocoa in hand, don't be surprised. I'm just making sure the magic never runs out.

You can connect with me on:

f https://www.facebook.com/guylaa

Also by Guyla Adams

From barnyards to beehives to brain fog I write with humor, heart, and a healthy dose of real life. Whether wrangling chickens, chasing focus, or drizzling wisdom (and honey) across the page, her books celebrate the beautiful chaos of learning, growing, and laughing through it all.

The Hen Commandments A witty, faith-filled look at life's lessons straight from the chicken coop. It's part inspiration, part chicken therapy, and all cluckin' good fun.

Get Organized with ADD — Equal parts honesty and humor, this guide offers practical, grace-filled tips for taming the whirlwind mind and turning "organized chaos" into actual progress.

The Buzzed & Blessed Series — A three-book romp through the sweet world of bees, honey, and all things sticky. From beginner beekeeping in *Buzz Basics*, to natural remedies in *Healing Honey*, to laugh-out-loud recipes in *Honey, Let's Eat!*, this series proves that life is better (and funnier) when it's a little messy and a lot sweet.

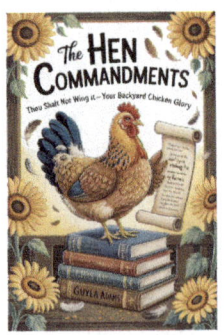

The Hen Commandments; Thou Shalt Not Take -Thy Chicken for Granted
Part hilarious handbook, part practical guide, this book delivers the gospel of backyard chickens with a wink and a cluck. From coop-building tips to egg recipes that'll make you shout "hallelu-yolk," it's everything you need to keep your flock happy—and yourself entertained. Warning: may cause sudden chicken adoption and excessive pun usage.

Buzz Basics: A Beginner's Guide to Beekeeping

Welcome to the hive, rookie! *Buzz Basics* is your hilarious, down-to-earth guide to starting beekeeping without getting stung—literally or figuratively. From setting up your first hive to understanding what your buzzing buddies are up to, this book breaks it all down with humor, heart, and a whole lot of honey. Perfect for beginners, dreamers, and anyone who's ever said, "I could totally keep bees... right?"

Your crash course in beekeeping—minus the confusion and plus a few laughs. Learn how to start, care for, and actually enjoy your hive with easy tips, honest advice, and stories stickier than fresh honey.

Get ready to hive, thrive, and survive your first year of beekeeping—with your sanity (and sense of humor) intact.

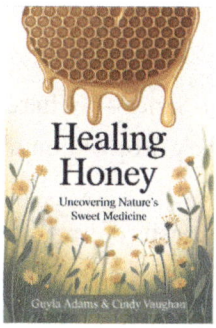

Healing Honey: Uncovering Nature's Sweet Medicine

Because Grandma—and the bees—were right all along. From soothing sore throats to softening skin, *Healing Honey* uncovers the sweet secrets of nature's most delicious medicine. Packed with down-to-earth wisdom, fascinating bee facts, and a dash of humor, this book will have you reaching for the honey jar instead of the medicine cabinet. Sweet, simple, and surprisingly scientific—your health has never tasted this good.

Sticky, sweet, and scientifically legit—this book explores all the wild and wonderful ways honey heals. From ancient remedies to modern uses, you'll learn why this golden goo deserves a spot in every kitchen (and first aid kit).

When life gets sore, scratchy, or just plain stressful, there's a bee-made cure for that.

Get Organized With Add; Techniques for Mastering Your Time

Unleash Your Inner Organization Guru and Master Time Management, Even If ADD Has Always Been Your Biggest Challenge!

Are you constantly battling clutter and chaos, feeling like a whirlwind of tasks and thoughts have taken over your life? Do you find yourself missing deadlines, battling procrastination, or overwhelmed by the mere thought of organizing your day? Does ADD feel like a relentless companion, always complicating your quest for a neat, orderly life? If you nodded along, you're definitely not alone. Many with ADD share these struggles, and it's time to turn the tables and reclaim control.

Honey Let's Eat; Cooking the Buzzed and Blessed Way

The Buzzed & Blessed Series

Welcome to *The Buzzed & Blessed Series* — where beekeeping meets belly laughs, and every drop of honey comes with a story.

Start with **Buzz Basics**, your crash course in beekeeping without losing your mind (or your bees).

Then dive into **Healing Honey**, uncovering nature's sweet medicine and all the sticky ways it can make life better.

Finally, feast your way through **Honey, Let's Eat!**, a hilarious, honey-soaked recipe adventure for every meal, mood, and midnight craving.

Whether you're here for the bees, the blessings, or just the snacks, this series proves one thing: life's sweeter when you keep it natural—and keep it funny.

Made in the USA
Coppell, TX
15 December 2025

65659117R00049